American edition published in 2021
by New Frontier Publishing Europe Ltd
www.newfrontierpublishing.us

First published in the UK in 2020
by New Frontier Publishing Europe Ltd
Uncommon, 126 New King's Rd, London SW6 4LZ, United Kingdom
www.newfrontierpublishing.co.uk

ISBN: 978-1-913639-13-6

Distributed in the United States and Canada by Lerner Publishing Group Inc.
241 First Avenue North, Minneapolis, MN 55401 USA
www.lernerbooks.com

Library of Congress Cataloging-in-Publication data is available.

Designed by Verity Clark

Printed in China
1 3 5 7 9 10 8 6 4 2

In My Dreams

For Dad—our dreams were filled
with possibilities
~ S G

For all who have saved
the inner child
~ T S

In My Dreams

Stef Gemmill & Tanja Stephani

NEW FRONTIER PUBLISHING

When the world is quiet and I'm alone,

I like to dream.

In my dreams, I can float

on marshmallow clouds,

splash in jelly puddles and showers of strawberry rain,

lick the stripes off rainbows, tasting the flavors of my favorite fruit.

In my dreams, I can dive deep

down to the ocean floor

and meet  creatures of the sea.

We chase fast fish for fun,

then race against pirates in dangerous seas.

They can't catch me.

In my dreams, I can fly on the back of my faithful dragon to faraway places.

We hunt with friends for treasure,

lining our pockets

with kisses and kindness

from the island of Love.

In my **dreams**, I can run with **wolves**.

Make mischief with monkeys.

Roar
with lions

and **leap** through a tangle of trees

with the pride at my side.

We dance around the fire

to the **beat** of the **drum.**

Boom-ba boom-ba boom!

In my dreams, I can ride the wildest winds,

seeking shelter from sleet and snow.

In the darkness,

the night shadows try to steal my sleep.

They have no power over me.

I can blink my eyes and they're gone.

In my dreams, I can see a warm light shining.

It sings my name and calls me home.

In my dreams, I am the brightest star in the wide universe.

Up here, I see a world I love and it loves me in return.

Reach for the **stars** in your **dreams** tonight.